W9-APX-932

TEN DOGS IN THE WINDOW

A Countdown Book by Claire Masurel
Illustrated by Pamela Paparone

North-South Books · New York · London

Text copyright © 1997 by Claire Masurel.
Illustrations copyright © 1997 by Pamela Paparone.
Published in the United States by North-South Books Inc., New York.
Published simultaneously in Great Britain, Canada, Australia, and New
Zealand in 1997 by North-South Books, an imprint of Nord-Süd Verlag AG,
Gossau Zürich, Switzerland.
First paperback edition published in 2000 by North-South Books.
Library of Congress Cataloging-in-Publication Data
Masurel, Claire.
Ten dogs in the window : a countdown book / by Claire Masurel ;
illustrated by Pamela Paparone.
Summary: After ten dogs are placed in a display window for the
whole wide world to see, one by one their numbers diminish until
the last canine departs with its new owner.
[1. Dogs—Fiction. 2. Pets—Fiction. 3. Counting.
4. Stories in rhyme.] I. Paparone, Pamela, ill. II. Title.
PZ8.3.M4215Te   1997
[E]—dc21   97-20945
A CIP catalogue record for this book is available from The British Library.
For more information about our books and the authors and artists who
create them, visit our web site: www.northsouth.com.
The artwork was created with acrylic paint.
Designed by Marc Cheshire. Printed in Belgium.
ISBN 1-55858-754-3 (trade binding) 10 9 8 7 6 5 4 3 2
ISBN 1-55858-755-1 (library binding) 10 9 8 7 6 5 4 3 2 1
ISBN 0-7358-1301-9 (paperback) 10 9 8 7 6 5 4 3 2 1

For Meg—CM
For Sam Dylan Overmyer—PP

10 dogs in the window for the whole wide world to see.
Look, someone is coming. . . .

"You're the perfect dog for me!"

9 dogs in the window for the whole wide world to see.
Look, someone is coming. . . .

"You're the perfect dog for me!"

8 dogs in the window for the whole wide world to see.
Look, someone is coming. . . .

"You're the perfect dog for me!"

7 dogs in the window for the whole wide world to see.
Look, someone is coming. . . .

"You're the perfect dog for me!"

6 dogs in the window for the whole wide world to see.
Look, someone is coming. . . .

"You're the perfect dog for me!"

5 dogs in the window for the whole wide world to see.
Look, someone is coming. . . .

"You're the perfect dog for me!"

4 dogs in the window for the whole wide world to see.
Look, someone is coming. . . .

"You're the perfect dog for me!"

3 dogs in the window for the whole wide world to see.
Look, someone is coming. . . .

"You're the perfect dog for me!"

2 dogs in the window for the whole wide world to see.
Look, someone is coming. . . .

"You're the perfect dog for me!"

1 dog in the window. She's as lonely as can be.

Look, someone is coming. . . .

And here's his family!

1 dog in the window. She is making such a fuss. Look, they all are stopping. . . .

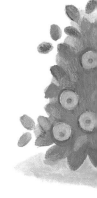

"You're the perfect dog for us!"